Haiku

For All

Seasons

by

Ruth Ann Allaire

Illustrated by

W. R. Michael Mattingly

and

Lisa Gay

Preface

Trapped by time and human frailty the author offers this book with contemporaneous musings on a life that is bound, usually by four walls, but with windows. The territory surveilled is five acres of suburban woods and a frequently visited farm. The interplay between plant and animal life gives meaning to the author. Author's means of perambulation.

A haiku captures

observations of the real

and inferences

Haiku goes dancing

in the strip joints of my mind.

Is nothing sacred

WINTER

A touch of pewter
cloaks tree branches to announce
winter has arrived

A dusting of snow
covers over weedy ground
camouflage begins

Doomsday predictions
are not for the lonely heart
already present

Winter sky turns white
letting white clouds slip inside
disappear from view

The red camellias
vie with cardinals today
for queen of color

No owl this morning
No birds fly by the window
Must I change my view

Little snow is left
to cover up last fall's weeds
More snow is needed

New ice on old grass
Rainbow sparkles in the sun
shine beautifully

Crows asked pecan tree
Why do you provide for us
nuts with worms inside

Last year's red berry
stands face-to-face with this year's
dogwood blossom bud

Robin foragers
seeking the bright red berries
settle for brown buds

Happiness itself
changes every minute
depending on view

Woodpecker on tree
by leaps ascends each morning
clinging on the bark

Gradually rain
erodes even the mountains
on way to oceans

The camellia said
Take your snowflakes and depart
after first white night

My bones belong here
beneath the tallest old trees
A place to call home

Dawn said to the sky
Good morning please embrace me
Til night said the sky

Nude branches shiver
as they sweep across the sky
looking for their leaves

Acrobatic leaps
define squirrel's morning jaunt
top of tree to top

Deer in the distance
foraging in underbrush
How close will they come

Silver is first light
before turning into gold
welcoming new day

Dilapidated
old wooden farm house still stands
Demolish or fix

When comes the morning
that pink camellia blossom
is not brown from frost

Last night's dark brown frost
hid camellia's white gown
That dance now over

A wintery walk
brings my old eyes to dried weeds
May turn green again

Snow on frozen ground
does not melt for many days
lasting until spring

When depression comes
arriving uninvited
barricade the doors

Once snow was promised
the children's hearts grew lighter
until Christmas rain

Branches fell today
crashing into silent ground
which replies with thud

What is blustery
When does wind become a gale
Too many questions

Crow calls his neighbor
safe from the night left behind
New call is raucous

Destructively wind
splinters the tree trunks and limbs
into mere kindling

Pink camellias
bring beauty soft and silent
to old opened eyes

In winter gloaming
the sky slides from blue to gray
losing all its light

Hungry chickadees
seek sustenance from black seeds
Danger all around

Impending snowstorm
brings thoughts of cocoa inside
Will there be enough

Gray is a splinter
The smallest fragment of dawn
through the blacker trees

How many branches
were lost on the way to growth
for very tall trees

Water shape shifters
Intricate design of flake
Ever changing sleet

Scraps of yesterday
make new quilts of memories
Comfort is at hand

Old leaves have fallen
Tree's structure can now be seen
Buds hold new design

Wind moving tree tops
appears to have no effect
on strong boles below

Rain sweeps white away
Dogwood petals are shrunken
Green is yet to come

Pink Christmas cactus
competes with poinsettia
for holiday cheer

Raccoon scratched the door
Pleading eyes looking up at me
How can I refuse

A slice of silver
between the black bread of trees
Another breakfast

Around the corner
she said talking of this spring
not the falling snow

Seasons come and go
Winter cannot last too long
or spring will not come

Seven days till spring
but daffodils are in bloom
Why don't they keep count

SPRING

Outside the window
the world beckons me anew
with fingers of spring

A soft sheet of green
blankets the sky with new leaves
as spring comes aboard

Fields of buttercup
bring the sunshine down to earth
Yellow becomes gold

Today new leaves dance
in remembrance of those
who have danced before

Inner core stays calm
while environment changes
Homeostasis

Space in the sky seen
between trees from my window
grows smaller each day

Lake rises again
Clambers over holding dam
Washes all away

With talons outstretched
osprey skims Rappahannock
searching for herring

Roosters competing
does not stop rain from pouring
all over the ground

Twisted white petals
tusks of dogwood mastodon
litter my landscape

Young fox at roadside
looks both ways turns to go back
Educated fox

Once was a lotus
of incredible beauty
which never did bloom

Energy flies low
gaining momentum at first
from far, far below

Single buttercup
brings yellow to the forefront
Fields soon followed suit

Her little finch died
This morning was different
No friendly chatter

Time said to all Grow
The acorn replied How fast
Relativity

With talons outstretched
the osprey dove down to snatch
fish from the river

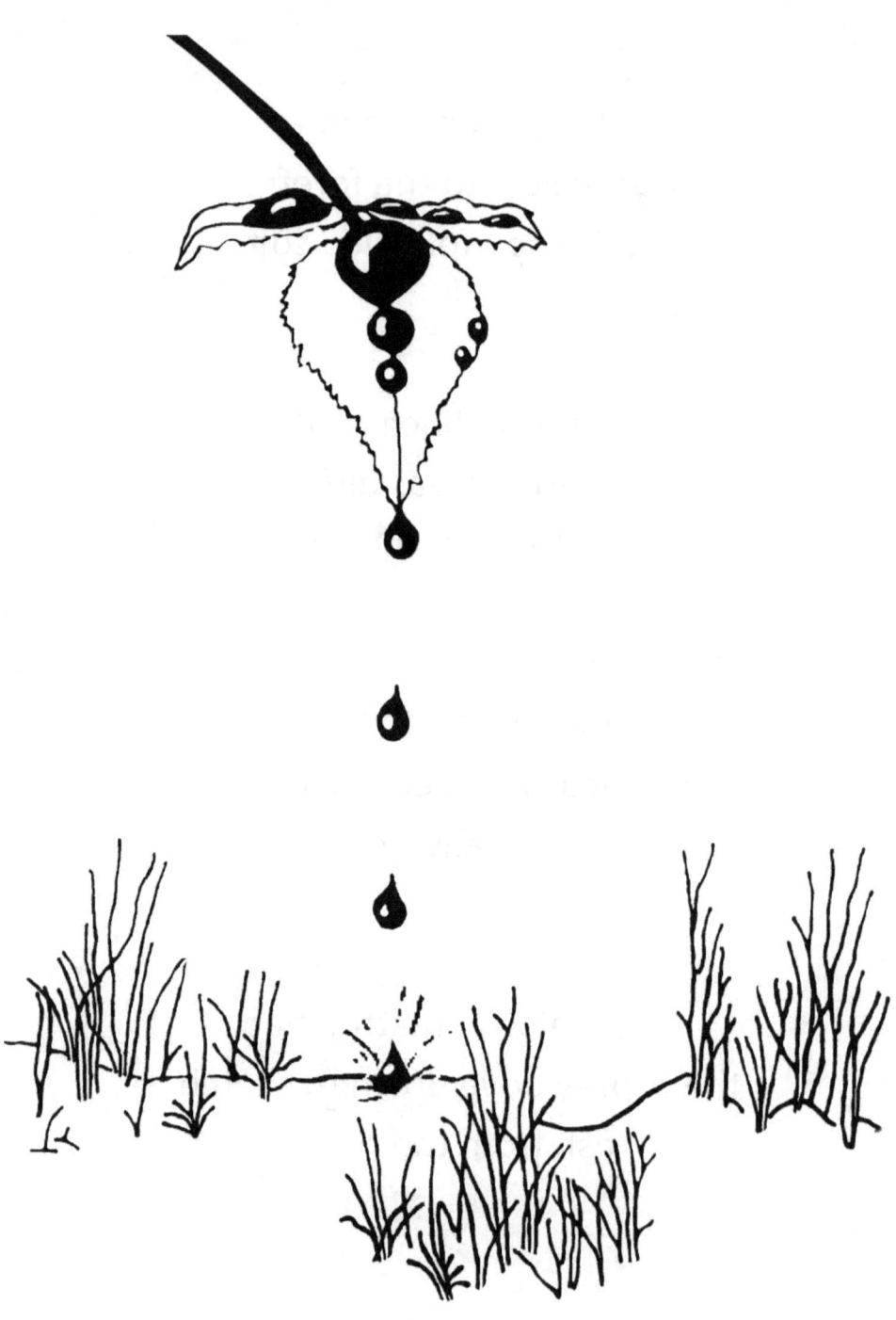

Where am I going
said raindrop sliding on leaf
Hard ground straight ahead

Female squirrel clings
tenaciously to branch
as male squirrel mounts

Tangential life
swipes back and forth over us
claiming any crown

Vultures circle round
a grim valley of despair
then leaflets appear

Rain pummeling earth
around newly planted trees
brings their salvation

Pendulous blossoms
offer up pecan pollen
in pale yellow clouds

Birds singing loudly
wake each and every day
to all perfection

Go to your brooding
said the rooster to the hen
It's time for babies

Pond of reflection
Haiku goldfish swimming by
Each one is precious

Which does singing bring
said cardinal to herself
Mate or hawk above

Yellow daffodil
as well as forsythia
bring sun to my eyes

Whippoorwill is loud
Her voice is sounding clearly
Whippoorwill again

What did daffodil
say to the old crocuses
Time's up now sweetie

Rooster says to dawn
Light gray is not your color
Must be rosy pink

New leaves in the trees
dance gracefully with the winds
Ballet in the sky

Tenants each morning
face eviction by nightfall
Always rooms to rent

Hawks rise with first light
advertising their presence
to those far below

Beavers eye alders
Saplings cry not me not me
One is soon chosen

What does rabbit hear
when fox is crossing the lawn
looking for breakfast

Sunlight shakes the day
leaves and trees and sky and earth
Wake up darling world

A tiny green leaf
growing bigger day by day
will soon block the sun

How green the mountain
overshadowing the fields
ready for the plow

First there was a tweet
then there was a tweety tweet
Rhapsody of tweets

Young tomato plant
close to the ground looked at sky
Must I go up there

Despite howling wind
tree holds its tremulous leaves
against warring night

Daffodil has died
yet lives on in ground below
fed by leaves above

One cannot go back
and change the trajectory
of those on the path

Groundhogs choose breakfast
Purple pansies eaten first
Tall grass for dessert

Morning has arrived
replete with bird song and light
Our hearts say welcome

How many green trees
uphold blue skies each morning
just to see color

Spring speaks with tulips
Language of beauty and bliss
Summer yet to come

Summer is coming
Temperatures are rising
Will there be blossoms

SUMMER

With early summer
Spring blossoms wither and die
escaping the heat

Summer steamy nights
No temperature dropping
Breath even hotter

Flowers said to sun
Lavish me with love and warmth
We will give beauty

Mornings come and go
Nape of neck of hummingbird
shows how green can glow

Shattering silence
Roosters' morning call begins
Rhythm of the Day

Crow call is harsher
than the sweet wren voice in life
yet stands still as true

Red tail says to Fox
Stay away Squirrels are mine
Have a nice rabbit

Cricket enters house
Chilly air forces this move
Chirping now begins

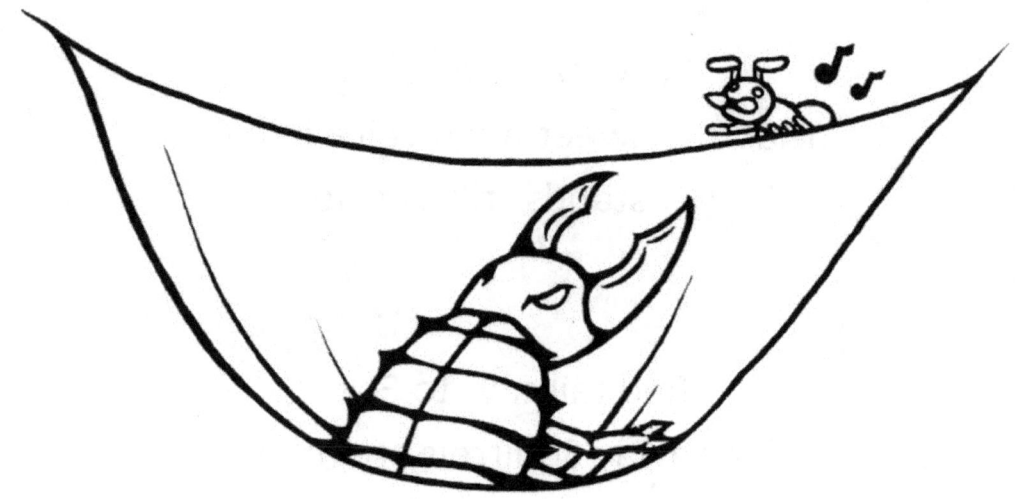

Doodle bug awaits
unwary ant to enter
the funnel of sand

Melodies differ
Inherent behavior songs
sing to each other

Something not quite right
Bald eagles standing in road
with turkey vultures

Hawk on windowsill
disoriented and lost
Far from sky above

Every vulture
is keen on day to begin
Aromas arise

Can we ever learn
how to navigate the world
without a pole star

Every morning
my eyes chase the rising sun
arc across the sky

What does rooster think
when the daylight first appears
Roll over and sleep

Pissants challenge hordes
with the insignificance
of even being

I asked Moon and Stars
Instead you gave me raw Earth
Build your own you said

Twilight slithers down
between trees seeking only
the gown of darkness

What must be added
to make vegetation be
a lovely garden

Esther the lone tree
stands guard over vast green space
washed with grass and weeds

In early June days
weather shifts from hot to cold
in terms of hours

Overheard hawk scream
Must be new generation
to announce presence

Let the rabbit jump
Horizon shows new clover
visible from air

Harmony occurs
when cacophony dies down
Music is a choice

A need for cool air
as temperatures rise up
Breeze even hotter

All occasion snake
One size fits all chicken eggs
Get yours tomorrow

Fox struts Rabbits hop
Groundhogs chew vegetables
Squirrels look for nuts

Raccoons stay at home
Opossum taking a nap
Deer just walks on by

Existence is now
This very second of time
Cannot ask for more

Fox said to red hawk
Squirrel is on your menu
I want the rabbit

Here in the farmyard
no bad karma is allowed
Just ask the chicken

Uneasy night times
elicit days full of hope
Mankind stays balanced

Opalescent sky
rises over mound of trees
Day can now begin

Lovely flowers
not at all wasted on weeds
Beauty is beauty

Chicken stealing fox
eyes naked woman with gun
Yields the battlefield

Hawk screeching above
says territory is mine
Enter if you dare

Dogs barking all night
eventually bring light
Need for fractured sleep

Wandering around
in the garden of my life
I try to pull weeds

Hear the Whippoorwill's
incessant call nearing dusk
welcome night again

Grasping the edges
of windows and doors alike
wren seeks a way out

At dark owls await
last call of the whippoorwill
Night music goes on

Breeze and misty rain
My spirit shivers thinking
darkness is coming

Fog horns or crickets
can shatter a quiet night
Just like a baby

Thunder beat the drums
calling rain drops to line up
and march across roof

Hummingbird air dance
provides field for mighty war
over food for life

Every season
light switches its duration
How long will mine last

Who would grow a weed
so intentionally
except for beauty

Midsummer noises
The cacophony of sound
overcome cricket

AUTUMN

World has turned yellow
covering yesterday's green
What hue tomorrow

Just now blossoming
late spring flower in the fall
Strawberries again

Within darkest night
Canada geese head homeward
Honks alone betray

Realization
Just a word to be pondered
or reality

I would call it bronze
the color red fox displays
to my aged eyes

Cricket noise is loud
Electricity is off
Are the sounds alive

At first streak of light
hawk screams in the silver sky
yet robin still sings

A door is a door
Separates space into rooms
apart from others

Bird feeders empty
Squirrels hunt diligently
for fallen pecans

Random flocks of geese
sound their noisy path across
a very still sky

Said cricket to ears
while chirping away at night
Small am I but loud

Chipmunk or squirrel
sagacity or cuteness
What price nuts these days

Leaves turning colors
sings a unique song as breath
escapes to the sky

Squirrel's mouth is full
The pecan has been engulfed
Cycles have their way

Gold covers my world
with wrinkled dying litter
Can such richness last

Yesterday was gold
Today is not tarnished yet
What price will be paid

Crows announce a prize
Tasty treasure deep within
Nuts are corvine gold

Tied up in small nuts
lie the genes for tomorrow
Mighty oaks to be

Life's challenge
just to face reality
as it faces us

Night creeps into view
causing bright light to abscond
in favor of dark

All is well Sky is
still blue Geese honk from that sky
Life goes on and on

Last year's leaves are gone
not discernible as such
New ones enter queue

Bird song fills the air
until a red hawk appears
Silence tells the tale

Hawk screamed I'm coming
Crow replied with his caw caw
So what big bad guy

I heard the rooster
calling back the dark of night
Sun rise up and shine

A minor discord
in the symphony of fall
Ninety-degree days

Rooster crows Last call
The loud-mouthed night crickets shout
The bar is now closed

Yesterday was gold
Today is still much the same
Ennui settles in

An unrecognized
bird language speaks through window
No time for glasses

Geese silhouetted
in shape of V as they fly
keep that formation

Surreptitiously
shades and shapes of absent trees
stand out in the dawn

Each hawk screams alone
Chickadee chats to neighbor
Eagle is silent

In early morning
night sounds mumble their goodbyes
Rooster claims the day

Morning said to crow
Is caw-caw your only word
Caw was the reply

Squirrel leaps from tree
The red hawk swoops down to grab
Near miss in the sky

Red hawk at sunrise
announcing to the sparrow
terror does still reign

At first crack of dawn
squirrel express starts to run
highest branches route

Two red-shouldered hawks
claim territory in sky
only one can stay

Single fallen leaf
facing far away bright sky
How here now from there

Whippoorwill stands guard
over the gateways to dusk
Calls to all who hear

Quiet cricket night
Comforted by steady drone
Shattered by sirens

My leaves are yellow
at their edge my leaves meet brown
Dying faces dead

Playing peek-a-boo
Moon slides between boles of trees
Beguiling night

Awaiting insight
into inner vibrations
we seek out our souls

Life is meaningless
to anguished Monarch enroute
Survival is best

Silver light swept sky
while feathers of dark black birds
scattered night away

On the thinnest branch
squirrel seeks another one
Fears not gravity

To find a new home
nut must leave tall tree and drop
straight to waiting ground

Little bit of snow
foretells the winter's magic
Quiet time ahead

Acknowledgements

Cover

Cover design and winter, spring, and summer photos
by Lisa Gay

Autumn photo
by Cathy Varner

Illustrations

Winter and Summer
by W. R. Michael Mattingly

Spring and Autumn
by Lisa Gay

Other Books by Ruth Ann Allaire

Rooms To Rent In The Relationship Hotels

Its Not Always Easy to Love A Drunk Or So It Is Said

More Rooms To Rent In The Relationship Hotels

Dialogues Between Two who tried to love and failing
that tried to share their inner dimensions

Still More Rooms To Rent In The Relationship Hotels

Winter in a River Beach Town

Tapestry of Grief

Love and Other Conundrums

Even More Rooms To Rent In The Relationship Hotels

Family Portrait

Whence The Quest, Whither and Why

Dragonflies in a Japanese Garden Pool

The Nature of Nature

Sketches of My Journey Through Life